Snow White

This book is dedicated to the first Charles Santore in our family, my father.

CHARLES SANTORE

Illustrations copyright © 1996 by Charles Santore.

This 1996 edition is published by Park Lane Press,
a division of Random House Value Publishing, Inc.,
40 Engelhard Avenue, Avenel, New Jersey 07001.

Park Lane Press and colophon are trademarks of
Random House Value Publishing, Inc.

Random House
New York • Toronto • London • Sydney • Auckland

Printed and bound in China

Book and jacket design by Kathryn Wolgast Plosica
Production supervision by Roméo Enriquez
Editorial supervision by Claire Booss and Nina Rosenstein

Library of Congress Cataloging-in-Publication Data

Schneewittchen. English.
    Snow White : a tale from the Brothers Grimm / illustrated by
Charles Santore.
        p. cm.
    Summary: Retells the tale of the beautiful princess whose lips were
red as blood, skin was white as snow, and hair was black as ebony.
    ISBN 0–517–20071–6
    [1. Fairy tales. 2. Folklore—Germany.] I. Grimm, Jacob, 1785–1863.
II. Grimm, Wilhelm, 1786–1859.   III. Santore, Charles, ill.   IV. Snow White
and the seven dwarfs. English.   V. Title.
PZ8.S415575 1996
[398.20943'02]—dc20   95–33734
                                                CIP
                                                 AC

8 7 6 5 4 3 2 1

Snow White

*A Tale from
the Brothers Grimm*

Illustrated by
Charles Santore

PARK LANE PRESS

New York • Avenel

nce upon a time, in the middle of winter, when the snowflakes were falling like feathers on the earth, a queen sat at a window framed in black ebony, and sewed. And as she sewed and gazed out at the white landscape, she pricked her finger with the needle, and three drops of blood fell on the snow outside. The red droplets showed so clearly against the white snow that she thought to herself, Oh, what wouldn't I give to have a child as white as snow, as red as blood, and as black as ebony!

Soon after, her wish was granted, and a little daughter was born to her, with skin as white as snow, lips and cheeks as red as blood, and hair as black as ebony. They named her Snow White. But not long after the child's birth, the queen died.

*a*fter a year, the king married
again. His new wife was a
beautiful woman, but so proud
and overbearing that she could
not stand any rival to her
beauty. She had a magic mirror,
and when she stood before it
gazing at her own reflection
she would ask:

"Mirror, mirror, on the wall,
Who is fairest of us all?"
The mirror always replied:
"Queen, you are fairest
of them all."
Then she was happy, for she
knew the mirror always spoke
the truth.

But Snow White was growing
prettier every day, and when she
was seven years old she was as
beautiful as the springtime,
and fairer even than the
queen herself.

One day when the queen asked her mirror the usual
question, it replied:

"My Lady Queen, you are fair, 'tis true,
But Snow White is fairer far than you."

Then the queen flew into the most awful rage, and
turned every shade of green in her jealousy. From
that hour she hated poor Snow White, and every day
her envy, hatred, and malice grew.

*a*t last, she could endure Snow White's presence no longer, and calling a huntsman to her, she said, "Take the child into the woods. You must kill her, and bring me proof that she is dead."

The huntsman had to obey his queen. He led Snow White out into the woods, but just as he was drawing out his knife to slay her, Snow White began to cry, and she said, "Oh, dear huntsman, spare my life, and I will promise to run into the wild forest and never return home again."

The huntsman paused for a moment. Then, because she was so young and sweet and pretty, he took pity on her, and said, "You are free to go, poor child." For he secretly thought that the wild beasts would soon eat her up. But his heart felt lighter, because he hadn't had to do the terrible deed himself. Then the hunter killed a young deer instead, and he brought the animal's heart to his queen as proof that he had carried out her evil command.

Now, when poor Snow White found herself alone in the big forest, she didn't know which way to turn, but she knew that she must run as far from the queen as she could go. There were so many strange noises in the forest—and the towering dark trees and their looming shadows looked fierce and ominous. She felt so frightened that she didn't know what to do, but she ran like the wind over sharp stones and through bramble bushes and across mountains. Sometimes the creatures of the wild darted right past her—bears and wolves and other beasts—but they did her no harm.

She ran as far as her legs would carry her, and as evening approached she saw a little house. Exhausted, she went inside to rest.

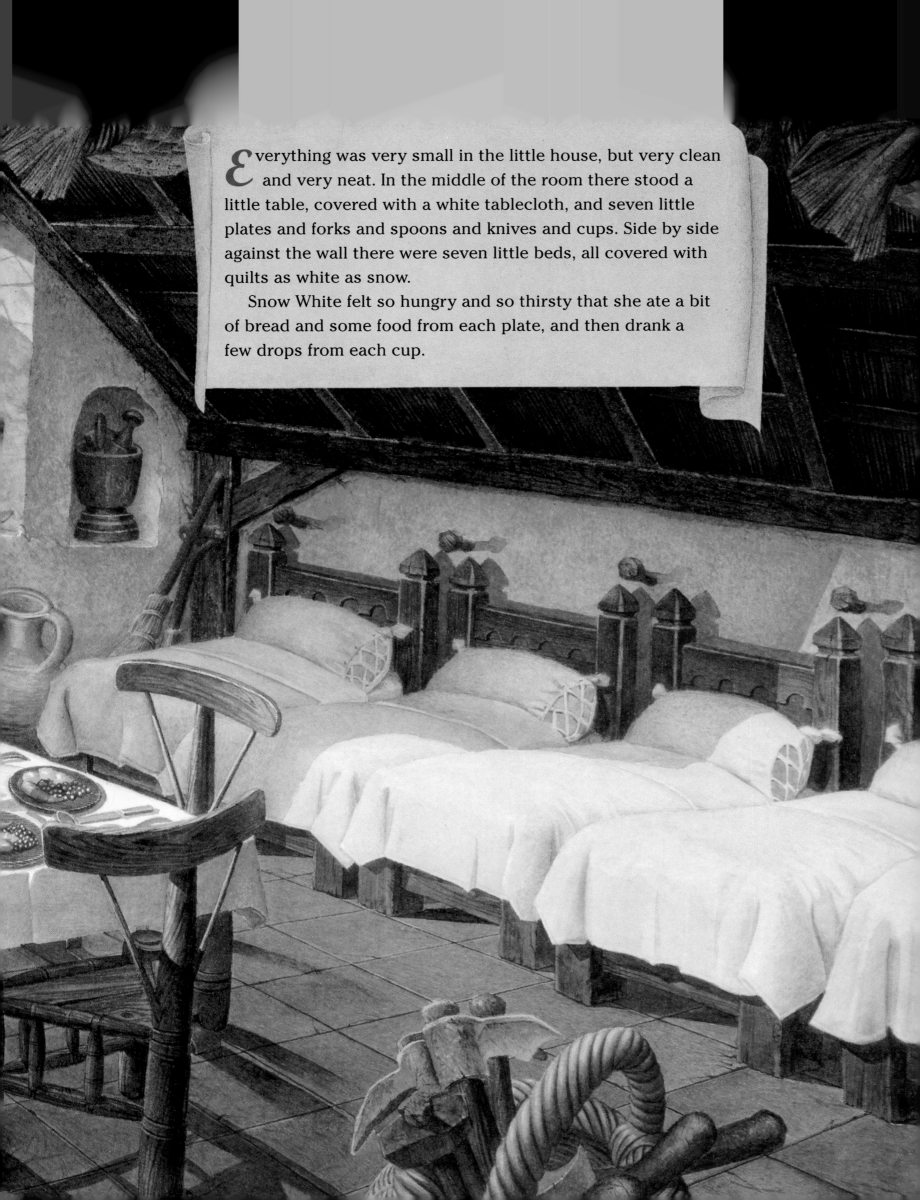

Everything was very small in the little house, but very clean and very neat. In the middle of the room there stood a little table, covered with a white tablecloth, and seven little plates and forks and spoons and knives and cups. Side by side against the wall there were seven little beds, all covered with quilts as white as snow.

Snow White felt so hungry and so thirsty that she ate a bit of bread and some food from each plate, and then drank a few drops from each cup.

Then, feeling tired and sleepy, she lay down on one of the beds, but it wasn't comfortable. So she tried all the others in turn, but one was too long, and another was too short, and it was only when she got to the seventh that she found a bed that was just right. So she lay down upon it and fell asleep.

When it got quite dark the owners of the little house returned. They were seven dwarfs who worked in the mines deep down in the heart of the mountain. They entered with their seven little lamps, and they soon saw that someone had been in the room.

The first dwarf said, "Who's been sitting in my chair?"

The second said, "Who's been eating my bread?"

The third said, "Who's been tasting my dinner?"

The fourth said, "Who's been eating out of my plate?"

The fifth said, "Who's been using my fork?"

The sixth said, "Who's been cutting with my knife?"

And the seventh said, "Who's been drinking out of my cup?"

Then the first dwarf looked around and saw a little hollow in his bed, and he asked, "Who's been lying on my bed?"

The others came running, and when they saw their beds, cried out, "Somebody has been lying on ours, too."

But when the seventh dwarf came to his bed, he jumped back in amazement, for there was Snow White fast asleep. So he called to the others, who came hurrying over. When they saw Snow White lying there, they gasped with surprise.

"Goodness gracious!" they cried. "What a beautiful child!"

They were so enchanted by her beauty that they did not wake her.
The seventh dwarf had to sleep with his companions one hour in each
bed, in order to get through the night.

In the morning when Snow White saw the seven little dwarfs she felt
very frightened. But they were so friendly and kind that she said, "Hello,
I am Snow White."

Then she told them how her stepmother had ordered her put to death,
and how the huntsman had spared her life, and how she had run the
whole day long till she had come to their house.

The dwarfs, when they heard Snow White's sad story, asked her, "Will you stay and keep house for us, cook, do the washing, sew, and knit? We could share our home with you and be your friends."

"Yes," answered Snow White. "I will gladly do all you ask."

And so she lived with them. Every morning the dwarfs went into the mountain to dig for gold, and in the evening when they returned home, Snow White always had their supper ready for them. But during the day the girl was left all alone, so the good dwarfs warned her, saying, "Beware of your stepmother. She will soon find out that you are here, and whatever you do, don't let anyone into the house."

*a*s soon as the queen got home she asked her mirror:
"*Mirror, mirror, hanging there,*
Who in all the land's most fair?"
And it replied as before:
"*My Lady Queen, you are fair, 'tis true,*
But Snow White is fairer far than you.
Snow White who dwells with the seven little men,
Is as fair as you, as fair again."
When the queen heard this she shook with fury.
"Snow White shall die," she cried. "Yes, though it cost me my own life."

Then she went to a secret chamber and prepared a poisonous apple. It looked beautiful and delicious, but anyone who took a bite would instantly die.

*I*nstead they made
a coffin of glass so they could continue to look at her, and
they wrote her name upon it in golden letters.

They carried the coffin to the top of the mountain, and from
that day on, one of the dwarfs always sat by her side. The birds
of the air came, too, and cried for Snow White. First came an
owl, then a raven, and last came a dove.

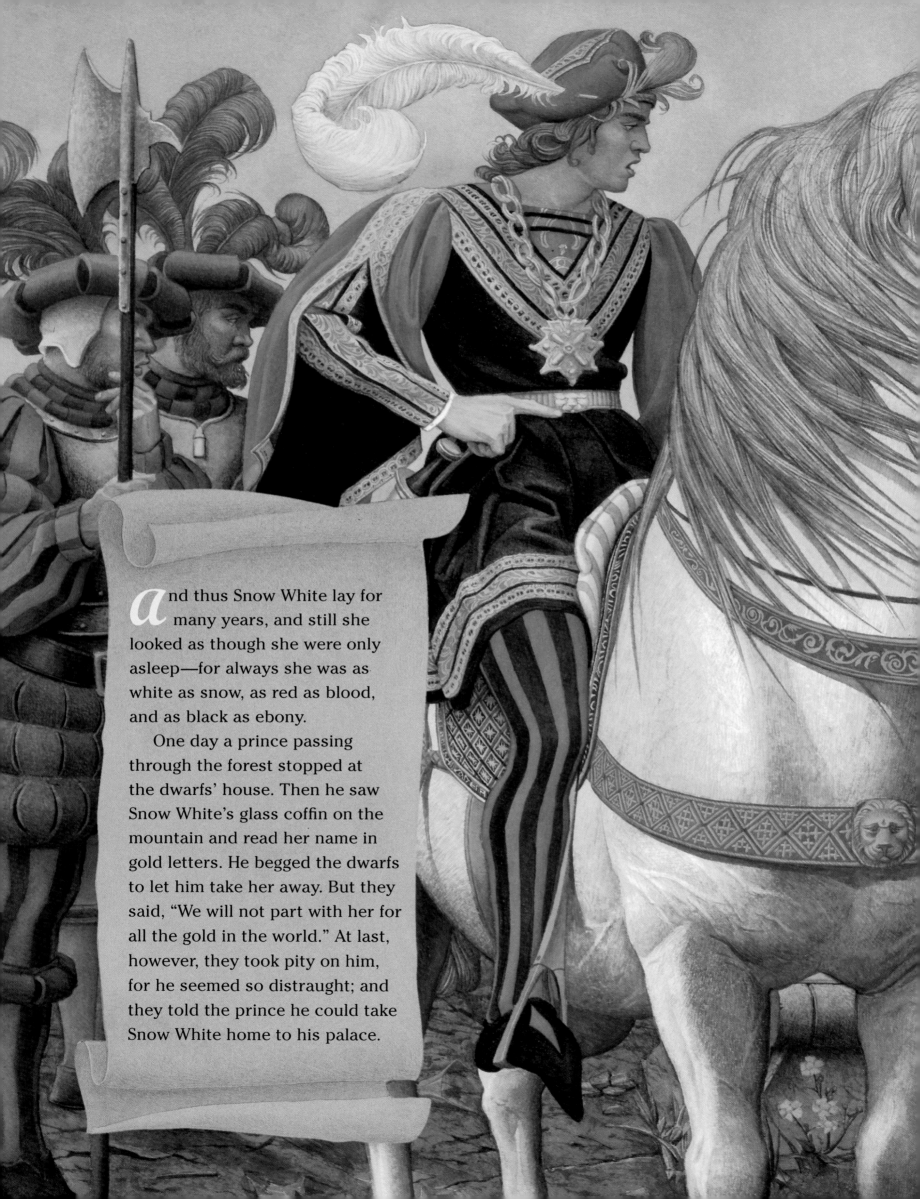

and thus Snow White lay for many years, and still she looked as though she were only asleep—for always she was as white as snow, as red as blood, and as black as ebony.

One day a prince passing through the forest stopped at the dwarfs' house. Then he saw Snow White's glass coffin on the mountain and read her name in gold letters. He begged the dwarfs to let him take her away. But they said, "We will not part with her for all the gold in the world." At last, however, they took pity on him, for he seemed so distraught; and they told the prince he could take Snow White home to his palace.

But the moment his servants lifted up the coffin, they stumbled and nearly dropped it. The jolt made the piece of poisoned apple fall from between Snow White's lips, and she instantly awoke, and asked, "Where am I? Who are you?"

The prince just smiled with joy. Then he told her all that had happened, and said, "I promise to love you better than all the world. Come with me to my father's palace, and you shall be my wife."

Snow White consented, and went home with the prince; and everything was prepared with great pomp and splendor for their wedding.

Everyone in the whole land was invited to the feast, even Snow White's old enemy, the wicked queen. As she was dressing herself in fine rich clothes, the queen looked in the glass and said:

"Tell me, mirror, tell me true!
 Of all the ladies in the land
 Who is fairest? Tell me who?"

And the glass answered:

"Queen, thou art fairest here, I hold,
 But the young queen is fairer, a thousandfold."

When the evil woman heard this, she shook with anger. But her envy and curiosity were so great that she could not help setting out to see the bride. And when she arrived, and saw that it was none other than Snow White, the queen was frozen with fright.

Then the wicked queen was commanded to put on a pair of magic slippers. The minute they were on her feet, the slippers forced her to dance and dance, faster and faster, until she dropped down dead.

There was great rejoicing in the hall, and Snow White and the prince lived in the palace and reigned happily over the land for many, many years.

About the Artist

CHARLES SANTORE has received numerous awards for artistic excellence, both for his past achievements in the magazine and advertising fields, and more recently for his illustrations for *Aesop's Fables, The Wizard of Oz,* and *The Little Mermaid,* which were published by JellyBean Press.

In 1992, he was honored for his work in book illustration with a major exhibition at the Brandywine River Museum. In addition, a selection of his paintings for *The Wizard of Oz* were used as the scenic backdrops for a major television performance of the work in 1995.

He lives and works in Philadelphia.